Uncle Sam's America

Uncle Sam

★ ★ ★

WRITTEN BY **DAVID HEWITT**

ILLUSTRATED BY **KATHRYN HEWITT**

★ ★ ★

To William Henry White,
born a slave and died a free man
—D. H.

To my grandmother Catherine Kroll,
who loved her adopted country and loved collecting stamps
—K. H.

SIMON & SCHUSTER BOOKS FOR YOUNG READERS ~ An imprint of Simon & Schuster
Children's Publishing Division ~ 1230 Avenue of the Americas, New York, New York 10020 ~
Copyright © 2008 by David Hewitt and Kathryn Hewitt ~ All rights reserved, including the right of
reproduction in whole or in part in any form. ~ SIMON & SCHUSTER BOOKS FOR YOUNG READERS is
a trademark of Simon & Schuster, Inc. ~ Book design by Jessica Sonkin ~ The text for this book is set
in Celestia Antiqua. ~ The illustrations for this book were created using mixed-media collage, oil paint,
and a variety of images from the Dover Clip-Art series. ~ Manufactured in China ~ 10 9 8 7 6 5 4 3 2 1 ~
Library of Congress Cataloging-in-Publication Data ~ Hewitt, David, 1949- ~ Uncle Sam's America /
by David Hewitt ; illustrated by Kathryn Hewitt. ~ p. cm. ~ ISBN-13: 978-1-4169-4075-3 (hardcover) ~
ISBN-10: 1-4169-4075-8 (hardcover) ~ 1. United States—History—Juvenile literature. 2. Uncle Sam
(Symbolic character)—Juvenile literature. 3. National characteristics, American—Juvenile literature.
I. Hewitt, Kathryn. II. Title. ~ E178.3.H58 2008 ~ 973—dc22 ~ 2007026530 ~ First Edition

sAMERICA

A Parade Through
— Our —
Star-Spangled History

SIMON & SCHUSTER BOOKS FOR YOUNG READERS
New York ★ London ★ Toronto ★ Sydney

BORN TRUE TO THE RED, WHITE, AND BLUE, Sam was always there to help his people. From the start he protected folks like a favorite uncle, so they called him Uncle Sam. Sam carried a flag adorned with stars, one for each state in America. Sam was bold and courageous defending his people—but it wasn't always easy.

LUCRETIA MOTT

Vermont   1791

Virginia   1788

Massachusetts   1788

THOMAS JEFFERSON
UNITED STATES
1¢

JOHN ADAMS

FOLLOWING THE REVOLUTIONARY WAR, Sam and the colonists
thought they were finished fighting the British Red Coats. But in 1812
the British showed up once more. They set fire to Washington, D.C.,
and that made Sam hoppin' mad. He knew just who to call for help—
General Andrew Jackson. Andy beat the Red Coats in New Orleans
and they never bothered Sam again. Sam inspired the people to
rebuild Washington, D.C., and from then on his countrymen
said he was bold, courageous, and kind.

BACK EAST things were getting pretty crowded, and folks needed space to spread out. Sam gazed west beyond the wide Mississippi and saw Kit Carson and other scouts exploring the hills and valleys ahead. Sam walked west with the pioneers, wearing out seven pairs of boots along the way—but when he got there he knew it was worth it. He was bold, courageous, and determined.

JUST AS SAM SAT DOWN to soak his tired feet in the cold Rocky Mountain streams, he heard a yell, "There's gold in them thar hills!" From the Black Hills of South Dakota to the Sierra Nevada in California, miners climbed over one another in search of gold. But to Sam, the joy of seeing his country grow was more precious than the gold the miners sought, and Sam was proud of each new state that added a bright star to his flag.

U.S.POSTAGE 4¢ LINCOLN

vada 1864

Kansas 1861

West Virginia 1863

Frederick Douglass

Harriet Tubman

AT THE SAME TIME, not all of the thirty-four stars on Sam's flag were shining so bright. Down South, some folks were getting rich by enslaving people from Africa. Sam saw his country falling apart and he didn't know how to fix it. The North battled with the South, and though they called this the Civil War, it sure wasn't very civil. Honest Abe Lincoln stepped forward. It was a true test of the nation, and many lives were lost on both sides of the Mason-Dixon line. But Sam and Abe were bold, courageous, and firm. With a lot of help from the American people, they saved the country, ended slavery, and put the shine back into Sam's stars.

1861 - 1865

JUST WHEN SAM THOUGHT he could take a break and enjoy a fresh Georgia peach, folks got itchy feet and began to look west again. Sam and many thousands of workers rolled up their sleeves, and their labor linked the Union Pacific and Central Pacific railroads together in Utah. Folks headed west in style to seek fame and fortune, though it was shame, misfortune, and a long trail of tears for many of the native people already living there.

Nebraska 1867

BAGGAGE

ACROSS THE COUNTRY, towns were springing up fast, and Sam was pleased to see the progress. Brand-new machines whirred and buzzed, and steam-powered ships filled the harbors with people looking for streets paved with gold. Life was sometimes hard and unfair, but like Uncle Sam, folks were bold, courageous, and unstoppable.

IN 1886 THE STATUE OF LIBERTY took her place in New York Harbor. At four hundred fifty thousand pounds and with a waist thirty-five feet around, she was hard to miss. She wasn't much like the fancy dressers in New York, but she had a heart as big as her feet (size 879). Her torch lit up the sky and put a gleam in Sam's eyes. Across the ocean, starvation and bickering among the leaders of Europe brought millions more people to our shores. They came looking for shelter, food, and a place to seek their dreams. Sam and Lady Liberty welcomed them all.

JULY
IV
MDCCLXXVI

1880s

Give me your tired,
your poor.

WITH ALL THESE NEW CITIZENS Sam wondered if he had enough land and clean water to offer everyone. Luckily for Sam, President Theodore Roosevelt loved our land too, and saw how important it was to protect our natural resources. The two of them were bold, courageous, and wise, creating national parks and wildlife areas so that folks would always have a place to enjoy the outdoors.

BY 1914 THE BICKERING IN EUROPE turned into full-fledged fighting. World War I was so bad they called it the war that would end all wars, but in 1918, after nearly five years and nine million lives lost, the war was over. Just as Sam began to catch his breath, then came the Great Depression, and depressing it was! Farms were wiped out by dust storms; people lost their money, their homes, and their jobs. Sam looked sadly across the land and said, "Who will stand with me?"

Oklahoma 1907

New Mexico 1912

Arizona 1912

John Steinbeck

APPLES 5¢

FEARLESS FRANKLIN D. ROOSEVELT, Teddy's cousin, came to the rescue. When the sky was at its darkest and stormiest, FDR told folks not to be afraid, that he and Uncle Sam would protect them. Together they built dams, roads, hospitals, and schools. They even created art for everyone to enjoy. Across the land Sam and FDR were known for being bold, courageous, and generous: putting workers back to work and watching over the poor and needy.

AT ABOUT THE SAME TIME some bullies called the Axis boys attacked Uncle Sam, and World War II began. Uncle Sam said, "Who will help me fight?" and people came from every direction all across the country. Rosie the Riveter built ships and planes, and soldiers named GI Joe marched with Sam to Europe and Asia to put an end to the Axis Powers. After the war the world was in a struggle to recover. Sam knew exactly what to do.

1941-1945

Norway

Sweden

Germany

Greece

Turkey

Austria

Harry S. Truman

U.S. Postage 8 cents

STATESMAN SOLDIER
GEORGE C. MARSHALL
20c
UNITED STATES

Italy

1947-1951

UNCLE SAM RALLIED AMERICANS to rebuild at home, and their efforts reached the rest of the world too. Though there would come other times when Uncle Sam would feel the need to wave a big stick in one hand, he became famous for sharing food and clothes, and helping people. He was bold, courageous, and giving.

BY THE TIME THE FLAG had fifty stars, America was so proud of its Uncle Sam that he became a symbol of the nation. Sam and his people were bold, courageous, and ambitious, and they worked hard to fulfill their dreams.

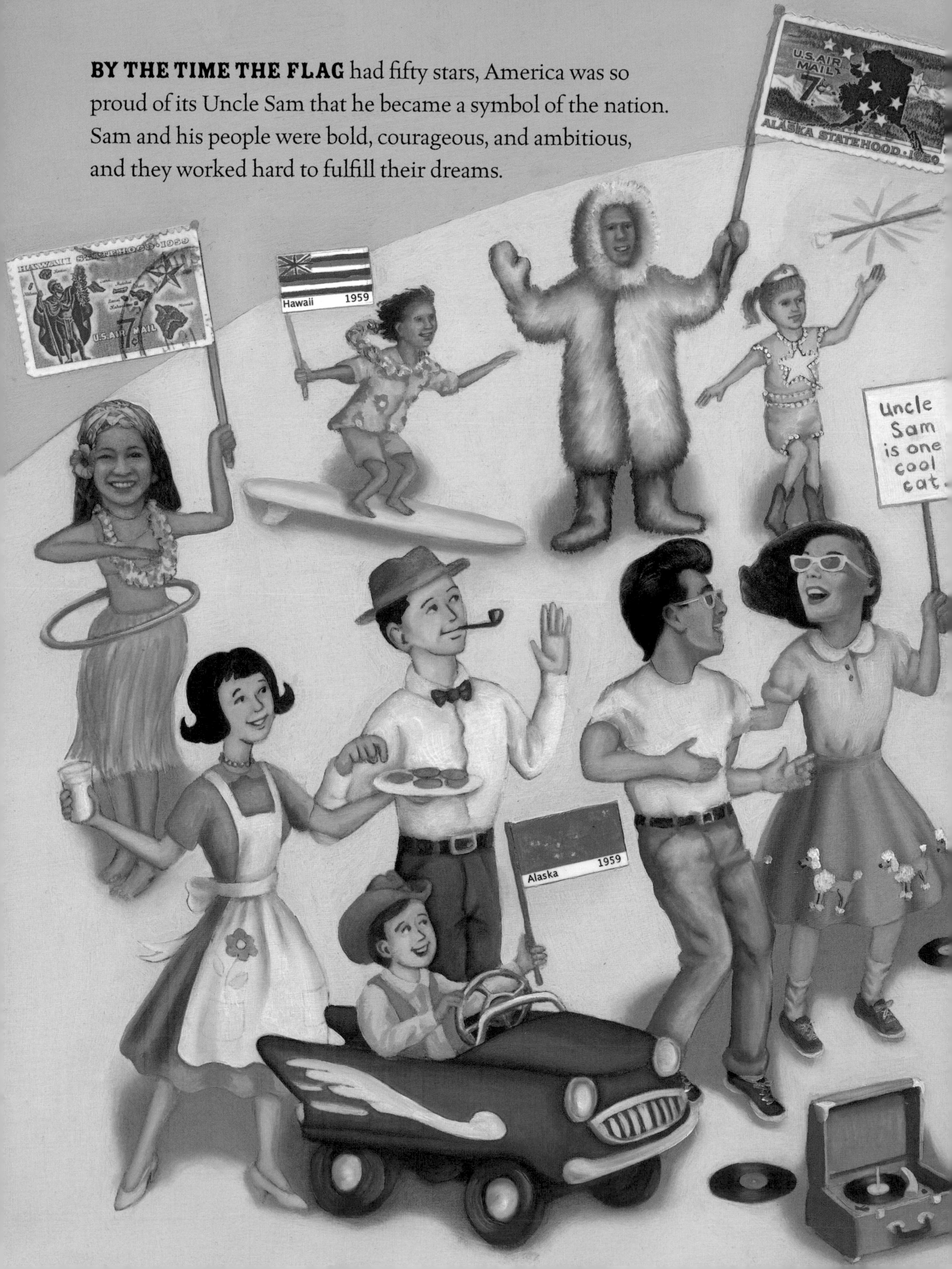

U.S. AIR MAIL
ALASKA STATEHOOD 1959
HAWAII STATEHOOD 1959
U.S. AIR MAIL
Hawaii 1959
Uncle Sam is one cool cat
Alaska 1959

Peace Corps
8c
United States

J. F. KENNEDY
13c
UNITED STATES

JACKIE ROBINSON

1950s

Civil Rights Act

Voting Rights Act — Lyndon Johnson

Ruby Bridges

BUT NOT EVERYONE had the same chances to achieve their goals. A man named Martin Luther King Jr. believed that all of America's citizens should have the right to make their dreams come true. Uncle Sam agreed and said, "Let's make sure that all people can vote. No one should be discouraged or mistreated because of their color or what they believe."

Rosa Parks

Brown v. Board of Education

Thurgood Marshall

Linda Brown

I'm sick and tired of being sick and tired.

A. Philip Randolph

Jobs & Freedom

Fannie Lou Hamer

1960s

GAZING ACROSS THE LAND, Sam knew that nothing was impossible, not even putting a man on the moon. Over the years Uncle Sam has been bold and courageous, helping to make America safe and prosperous. But for every accomplishment, great and small, Uncle Sam has never done it alone.

UNITED STATES POSTAGE

½ CENT

WASHINGTON

Benjamin Banneker

UNITED STATES POSTAGE

5 CENTS

LOUISA MAY ALCOTT

Cesar Chavez

NO MATTER WHAT THE CHALLENGE, Sam and the American people march boldly and courageously forward, realizing dreams of the past and carrying a message of kindness and hope for the future.

Chief Joseph

VOTE

George Washington Carver

AUTHOR'S NOTE

Although fictional, Uncle Sam is claimed to be based upon an actual person. Samuel Wilson worked as a meat inspector and was the nephew of a man who supplied the army with salt pork and beef during the War of 1812. Inspectors stamped barrels of meat with the initials U.S., which indicated the shipment was for the United States government. At the same time, some people who opposed the war used the name Uncle Sam as a derogatory term for the United States federal government. The link between Wilson and the name Uncle Sam stuck. Wilson died in Troy, New York, in 1854, at the age of eighty-eight. In 1961 Congress adopted a resolution saluting Uncle Sam Wilson and recognizing Uncle Sam as America's national image. Accordingly, while history reveals our mistakes as well as our past glories, Uncle Sam, like most of us, remains a work in progress.

ACKNOWLEDGMENTS

The Hewitts are indebted to Paula Wiseman, Alyssa Eisner Henkin, Elizabeth Law, and especially Alexandra Cooper, Jessica Sonkin, and the inspiration and champion of Uncle Sam—Rubin Pfeffer.

★ ★ ★ FAMOUS AMERICANS ★ ★ ★

John Adams (1735–1826) First vice president, second president, helped write the Declaration of Independence.

Louisa May Alcott (1832–1888) Writer best known for *Little Women* and other books for children.

Susan B. Anthony (1820–1906) Worked against slavery and for women's rights.

John J. Audubon (1785–1851) Artist, ornithologist who painted all the known species of birds in nineteenth-century America.

Benjamin Banneker (1731–1806) African-American scientist, mathematician, astronomer, clock maker, and surveyor of Washington, D.C.

Elizabeth Blackwell (1821–1910) First woman doctor in the United States.

Ruby Bridges (1954–) Pioneer of school desegregation at age six.

Linda Brown (1943–) As a third grader, participated in *Brown v. Board of Education* action against segregated schools.

Kit Carson (1809–1868) Guide in western expeditions, soldier.

George Washington Carver (1864–1943) Botanist, chemist, former slave.

Cesar Chavez (1927–1993) Founder of first successful farm workers union.

Frederick Douglass (1817–1895) Abolitionist, newspaper publisher, lecturer.

George Eastman (1854–1932) Inventor who founded Kodak Co.

Thomas Edison (1847–1931) Inventor of telephone, lightbulbs, phonograph.

Albert Einstein (1879–1955) Physicist, awarded Nobel Prize in 1921.

Ben Franklin (1709–1790) U.S. inventor, diplomat, statesmen.

Fannie Lou Hamer (1917–1977) Worked for voting rights in the 1960s.

Andrew Jackson (1767–1845) General, lawyer, senator, judge, and seventh president.

John Jay (1745–1829) First Chief Justice of Supreme Court.

Thomas Jefferson (1743–1826) Third president, architect, inventor, botanist.

Lyndon Johnson (1908–1973) Teacher, senator, vice president, and thirty-sixth president.

Chief Joseph (1840–1904) Native American Chief of the Nez Perce.

John F. Kennedy (1917–1963) Naval hero, senator, thirty-fifth president.

Martin Luther King Jr. (1929–1968) Clergyman, civil rights leader who practiced nonviolence.

Abraham Lincoln (1809–1865) Lawyer, sixteenth president, signed the Emancipation Proclamation.

George Marshall (1880–1959) Army Chief of Staff in WW II, awarded Nobel Prize for European Recovery Program (Marshall Plan).

Thurgood Marshall (1908–1993) Supreme Court Justice, civil rights advocate.

James Monroe (1758–1831) Fifth president.

Lucretia Mott (1793–1880) Quaker, worked against slavery and for women's rights.

Rosa Parks (1913–2005) Called mother of the civil rights movement for refusing to move to the back of a bus.

George Patton (1885–1945) Military officer in World War II.

A. Philip Randolph (1889–1979) Labor leader, civil rights worker, organizer of March on Washington for Jobs and Freedom in 1963.

Paul Revere (1735–1818) Patriot, silversmith, printer, most famous for his ride warning the British were on the march.

Jackie Robinson (1919–1972) First African-American to play in major leagues.

Eleanor Roosevelt (1884–1962) Humanitarian, first lady, U.N. ambassador.

Franklin Roosevelt (1882–1945) Thirty-second president, elected four terms.

Theodore Roosevelt (1858–1919) Twenty-sixth president, Rough Rider, author.

John Steinbeck (1902–1968) Writer, won Pulitzer Prize for *The Grapes of Wrath*.

Harry S. Truman (1884–1972) Farmer, senator, vice president, and thirty-third president.

Harriet Tubman (1820–1913) Former slave who led over three hundred slaves to freedom, nurse; only woman to lead troops in the Civil War.

Mark Twain (1835–1910) (Samuel Clemens) Wry humorist who wrote books about American life: *The Adventures of Huckleberry Finn, The Adventures of Tom Sawyer.*

George Washington (1732–1799) Surveyor, general, first president.

Walt Whitman (1819–1892) Poet, Civil War nurse.